THE PIRATE-CRUNCHER

Lubbers' Land

Clarendon

St. Andrew

The

St. David

54

51

50

Inner Harbour

Port Royal

Bull Bay

Galleon Harbour

Half Moon Bay

Cow Bay

Monkey Bay

Scurvy Sands

Wreck Bay

Cutlass Point

Fiddle Bay

Yarmini's Head

Grundy Head

19

Fish Head

Blubber Bay

Grisly Head

18

Peak Bay

17

There Be
TREASURE
Abroad!

16

15

11

oooOoo-AaaARR!

Ye Wavy Bit...

Doubloon Bay

Pirate Point

Monster Hole

Puppet Point

Parrot Point

Rude to Point

Swamp!

Rocky Point

Toothy Point

tains

Watch out for
MONSTERS!

Here Be
Treasure!

oOoo-aaAR!

Get it QUICK before
some other PIRATES do!!

My dear fellow pirate,

Do ye want to be RICH?
To get TREASURE beyond yer wildest dreams —
to find nuggets of GOLD as big as ships' beams?
And DIAMONDS and RUBIES
the size of yer eyes!
Just follow this MAP (please see reverse)
to claim yer PRIZE.*

From a friend x x x

*conditions apply

For Dad, because I know
you would have been proud – J.D.

A TEMPLAR BOOK

First published in the UK in 2009 by Templar Publishing.
This softback edition with audio CD published in the UK in 2011
by Templar Publishing, an imprint of The Templar Company Limited,
Deepdene Lodge, Deepdene Avenue, Dorking, RH5 1AT, UK
www.templarco.co.uk

Copyright © 2009 by Jonny Duddle

Second softback edition, fourth impression

ISBN 978-1-84877-378-3

Edited by Libby Hamilton

Printed in Turkey

All was unusually quiet
in Port Royal...

but if you listened carefully, on the quayside,

Thirsty

Parrot

you could hear the
faint sound of a fiddle
floating on the wind.

down the alleyways
and in the candlelit taverns,

Outside the Thirsty Parrot Inn, an old fiddler appeared. As he fiddled, he sang a song...

"I WAS SAILING ONE DAY AND WHAT DID I SEE?
AN ISLAND OF GOLD IN THE SCURVY SEA!
WITH A FIDDLE-DE-DEE,
THERE'LL BE TREASURE FOR ME.
FIDDLE-DE-DEE, ACROSS THE SEA."

His shanty caught the ear of the dastardly Captain Purplebeard. Putting down his ale and wiping his lips, Purplebeard bellowed out the window...

The fiddler unfurled
his map and sang:

"I'LL SHOW YE MY MAP IF YE'LL TAKE ME THERE –
THERE'LL BE TREASURE ENOUGH
FOR US ALL TO SHARE!"

The Captain smiled and said, "By thunder!
That sounds just like our sort of plunder
or my name ain't Pirate Purplebeard of Penzance.
Finish your grog lads – WE SET SAIL AT ONCE!"

The sun was coming up as Captain Purplebeard and his cut-throat crew boarded their ship, the BLACKHOLE. Behind them came the old fiddler, still dancing and singing:

"TO FIND THIS ISLAND, YOU'LL HAVE TO BE QUICK - FOR THEY SAY IT PERFORMS A VANISHING TRICK! AND NONE WHO'VE TRIED TO SET FOOT ON ITS SANDS, HAVE EVER RETURNED TO PIRATE LANDS."

But the Captain just sneered, "What NONSENSE, I say."

ALL ABOARD ME HEARTIES

So off they sailed across the sea. And as they tucked into breakfast, the old fiddler began again:

"THERE IS ONE SMALL THING I FORGOT YESTERDAY –
THERE'S ALSO A MONSTER, OR SO THEY SAY.
HE LIKES TO EAT PIRATES WHO COME FOR HIS TREASURE,
AND HE CHEWS UP THEIR SHIPS,
JUST FOR GOOD MEASURE."

"YOU SCURVY SEA DOG!" bellowed the Captain.

"Be it MADE-UP or MONSTROUS, it's no match for me.

I'm Captain Purplebeard.

SCOURGE of the SEA!"

And the fiddler said:

"OH YES, I AGREE,
HE DOESN'T **SCARE** ME!

THOUGH, NO BONES ABOUT IT;
HE'S A **BIG** OLD BEAST,

WHO LIKES NOTHING MORE
THAN A PIRATE FEAST.

HE CAN SWALLOW WHOLE SHIPS
IN HIS WHIRLPOOL JAWS
(THOUGH THEY SAY HE'S ALLERGIC
TO SCARLET MACAWS)."

"THERE ARE RUBIES AND DIAMONDS
THE SIZE OF BALLOONS –
SILVER AND GUINEAS
AND GOLDEN DOUBLOONS.
BUT GRAB IT ALL QUICK
OR HE'LL HAVE YOUR ENTRAILS!
NOW, FIDDLE-DE-DEE, LET'S
SPREAD THOSE SAILS."

But no one moved
on the deck below.
The crew looked
around in FEAR
and DREAD,
as visions of
monsters filled
their heads...

"GO HOME?!"
roared Captain Purplebeard.
"I'll keelhaul you all, you
cowardly landlubbers.
The ONLY thing YOU need to
be frightened of is ME!"

So with visions of monsters in EVERY head,
the motley old crew trudged off to bed.
Most had nightmares and TERRIBLE dreams
and the hold was full of pirate SCREAMS.

But up on the poop deck the captain was HAPPY,
for HIS head was full of dreams about treasure...
"GOLD or SILVER, I don't care which,
just as long as it makes me filthy RICH!"

Next morning, the crew were worried.
They couldn't be sure, but the day before
it seemed that they had numbered more...

and the fiddler told them:
IF YOU'RE TOO SCARED, TURN BACK TO PORT.
YOU'RE HAPPY AND HEALTHY, BUT FOR SCURVY AND WARTS.
IT'S SAFER BY FAR TO RETURN TO SHORE,
AND AS FOR THE TREASURE,
DO YOU REALLY NEED MORE?"

"SHIVER ME TIMBERS!" laughed Captain Purplebeard.
"You should know by now that never, EVER
can any pirate have ENOUGH treasure.
And if there's a BEAST, it'd better BEWARE.
I can SMELL that gold! We're nearly there!"

Just then, from up in the crow's nest, there came a call...

LAND AHOY!

"HURRAH!" yelled the pirates, forgetting their fear, now the promise of treasure was so VERY near.

As they clambered ashore,
no one saw a thing wrong –
too busy to heed
the fiddler's
last song...

Lubbers' Land

Clarendon

St. Andrew

The

St. David

Inner Harbour

Port Royal

Bull Bay

Half Moon Bay

Galleon Harbour

Scurvy Sands

Wreck Bay

Cow Bay

Monkey Bay

Cutlass Point

Fiddle Bay

Varmint's Head

Fish Head

Bubbler Bay

Groggy Head

Grundy Head

Peak Bay

There Be TREASURE Abroad!

oooOoo-AaaARR!

Ye Wavy Bit...

A salty cove, Jonny Duddle
overheard the story of his first book,
THE PIRATE-CRUNCHER, while sailing in a square-rigger.
Then, in a quiet seaside town, he found an even stranger tale,
THE PIRATES NEXT DOOR, which has won the Waterstones
Children's Book Prize and become a best-seller.

Now in danger of becoming a landlubber,
Jonny lives in Wales with his wife Jane and
their daughters, Daisy and Rosie.